I0669706

William James Hoge

Sketch of Dabney Carr Harrison

Minister of the gospel and captain in the army of the Confederate States

of America

William James Hoge

Sketch of Dabney Carr Harrison
Minister of the gospel and captain in the army of the Confederate States of America

ISBN/EAN: 9783337083465

Printed in Europe, USA, Canada, Australia, Japan

Cover: Foto ©Raphael Reischuk / pixelio.de

More available books at **www.hansebooks.com**

SKETCH OF

DABNEY CARR HARRISON,

Minister of the Gospel

AND

CAPTAIN IN THE ARMY

OF THE

CONFEDERATE STATES OF AMERICA.

BY WILLIAM J. HOGE, D. D.

AUTHOR OF BLIND BARTIMEUS.

RICHMOND:

PRESBYTERIAN COMMITTEE OF PUBLICATION
OF THE CONFEDERATE STATES.

1862.

DABNEY CARR HARRISON,

SOLDIER OF THE CROSS AND OF HIS COUNTRY.

BY WILLIAM J. HOGE, D. D.

This faithful minister of Christ, this noble gentleman and valiant officer, fell at Fort Donelson, while cheering on his men, and striking for the honor and independence of our young Confederacy.

At the request of judicious friends, I have prepared this brief narrative for circulation in the army. "My heart's desire and prayer to God" for all my readers is, that they may have "like precious faith" with him. I can not wish them a more beautiful and blessed life, nor a death more peaceful and full of glory.

He was born in the county of Albemarle, Virginia, on the 12th of September, 1830. His father, the Rev. Peyton Harrison, still lives; but his mother, Jane Cary Carr, daughter of Judge Dabney Carr, was mercifully "taken away from the evil to come."—Her soul, so rich in genius and culture, so quick and large in its sympathies, and so capacious of suffering, rested from its labors

and slept in Jesus, before the tempest burst
upon her country, her State, and her own
happy household.

Capt. Harrison was descended, on either
side, from sturdy patriots. He was the kins-
man of two of the signers of the Declaration
of Independence. One of them was its il-
lustrious author; the other was the father of
President Harrison. I shall be pardoned
for devoting a few lines to the memory of
his great-grandfather, Dabney Carr, especially as this association of names serves to
draw our first great Revolution and our second into closer relation. He had the honor
of bringing forward in the House of Bur-
gesses, A. D. 1773, a measure for the crea-
tion of what Mr. Wirt calls "that powerful
engine of resistance,—corresponding committees between the legislatures of the different colonies." Though but twenty-nine
years of age, he "was considered," says the
same high authority, "by far the most form-
idable rival in forensic eloquence that Patrick Henry had ever yet had to encounter."
He describes "his devotion to the cause of
liberty" as "verging on enthusiasm," while
"his spirit" was "firm and undaunted, beyond the possibility of being shaken."

His career, too, was brief as it was bril-
liant. He died in Charlottesville, Sunday,

May 16th, only two months after this auspicious entrance into his country's public service.*

I now return to the immediate subject of this sketch.

From early childhood he was remarkable for thoughtfulness, integrity, self-denial, perseverance in difficult undertakings, and unfailing obedience to his parents. He cherished to his dying day a little silver coin, with these words, "To an obedient son," inscribed on it with a pen-knife by his father. It was given on an occasion when he had, without hesitation, obeyed a request involving no little sacrifice of boyish pride and prejudice. His studiousness very early gave promise of the rich acquisitions of his after life. When but nine years old he read, in his play hours, the whole of Hume's History of England. During his childhood his parents adopted the plan of paying their children for abstaining from some of the delicacies of the table, for the sake of the heathen. The goodly sum which little Dabney brought forth, year by year, as the agent for Foreign Missions made his round, and the honest pleasure with which he gave it, bore witness how heartily and patiently he could deny himself for others' need. His favorite

* Wirt's Life of Patrick Henry, pp. 89, 90.

books, his compositions, and his conscientious walk and conversation, show that the whole tendency of his mind was, even at this period, deeply religious.

When just fifteen, he entered the Sophomore class in Princeton College, though his preparation was in advance of what was required. After an unusually blameless and honorable course at this institution, he began the study of the Law with a relative in Martinsburg, and pursued it at the University of Virginia for two years. He then returned to Martinsburg, and entered on the practice of this profession.

He was well fitted for it both by nature and education. His memory was quick, tenacious and prompt; so that his acquisitions were rapidly made, firmly held, and always at command. His understanding was comprehensive and solid; while his imagination, without being vivid, was graceful and chaste. His perception was keen, his judgment cool, his language clear. He had singular facility in explanation. No one could impart information more pleasantly. He charmed you on toward knowing what he knew, without once making you blush because you did not know it before. His historical and political knowledge was copious and accurate. Having an intrepid intellect, he was fond of discussion. Incapable of artifice himself, he was yet not easily entrapped by an opponent. At this period of his life, his speech was, I fear, too often sarcastic; but after grace began its reign, his wit grew constantly softer, and survived, at length, in the form of good-humored pleasantry only, played off upon friends who could understand and enjoy it.

His emotions were ardent, but under strong control. He had ready sympathies for the weak, generous indignation for the injured, while for purity and honor, for liberty and right, he was full of noble enthusiasm.

He had, moreover, the advantages of a pleasing address, classic features, a serene and contemplative countenance, the frankness of a fearless and cordial nature, and the manners of a thorough gentleman.

With such qualifications, and with a glowing ambition, he entered on his professional career.

But "man's goings are of the Lord: how can a man, then, understand his own way?" He can not. He may, indeed, "devise his way: but the Lord directeth his steps."

So it was here. Other and higher work had been marked out in heaven for this young lawyer, though as yet he knew it not.

He was to be "an ambassador for Christ," having in trust "the glorious gospel of the blessed God."

An event which came to pass in his early childhood was, no doubt, an important link in the providential chain by which he was now drawn. While yet a little boy, he had seen his father give up the legal practice he had been acquiring for years, and remove, with all his family, to the Theological Seminary, that he might learn to preach Christ, and be henceforth a servant of the saints for Jesus' sake. How constantly was that household ever after taught that, for a man redeemed from sin, and called of God, the ministry of the gospel is the noblest of all employments, the sweetest of all privileges, and the richest of all means of usefulness! With what importunity did his parents pray that God would choose, some, at least, of their sons, and "count them faithful, putting them into the ministry!"

At length, in the case of this son, God's time drew near. The Holy Spirit began to trouble his heart anew, as He had done several years before. The death, about this time, in her youthful bloom, of a favorite cousin, who had been the intimate companion of his social and literary pleasures, greatly increased the gracious movement which God had revived in his soul. The vanity and uncertainty of life, the solid glories of the things which though unseen are eternal, the claims of God, and the needs of his own soul and of his dying fellow-men, were continually before him. In his long, lonely walks and rides, he "pondered these things in his heart," and at length, by the grace of God, he gave himself, at once and forever, wholly and unreservedly to God and His blessed service. He abandoned the Law, and entered immediately on the study of Theology ; first under the guidance of his father, and then at Union Seminary. Here he enjoyed the inestimable instructions of Dr. Sampson. Their minds and hearts were most congenial, and his affection for his accomplished and heavenly-minded professor was reverential and enthusiastic. It' is sweet to think of them now, reunited in the study of that glorious and inexhaustible Word, into whose hidden treasures they searched so ardently on earth.

While he had still a year of his Seminary course before him, Dr. Sampson's death occurred; but the "profiting" of his loving pupil had so "appeared to all," that he was immediately appointed to conduct the stu_ dies of a considerable portion of the difficult department now made vacant. He spent two years in these labors, delighting the students and giving satisfaction to all.

But notwithstanding his "aptness to teach," his devotion to oriental learning, and his rare skill in the Hebrew, his heart still yearned for the peculiar work of the Gospel ministry. For nine months he acted as pastoral supply to the College Church, at Hampden Sidney, and for six months more he sustained this relation to the First Presbyterian Church in Lynchburg.

A still wider field now opened before him. He was chosen to be chaplain of the University of Virginia. In this office he endeared himself to the whole community, gained the confidence and good-will of the vast body of students, and "won golden opinions" from men whose commendation is praise indeed. One of those eminent Professors has been heard to say, "I never knew a more successful copy of the life of our Saviour than his." Another said, "I knew him intimately. Our conversation was as unguarded as that of brothers; and every sentiment I ever heard him utter was worthy of a gentleman and a Christian. I never knew him to neglect a duty, or even to postpone one. He was always faithful to his country, and faithful to his God."

It adds weight to these encomiums to re-

flect how delicate and difficult are both pulpit and pastoral labors among more than six
hundred University students. During this
time, too, for some months, the typhoid fever
raged among them with fearful power. Early
and late he was found at his post, by the
bedside of the sick and dying, ministering
with unwearied tenderness, both to body and
soul. He had his reward in their gratitude
and love, and often in evidences of their con-
version or spiritual edification.

Just as his term of service at the University
expired, he was summoned to "Clifton," that
beautiful old homestead, the abode of refine-
ment and piety and elegant hospitality, and
for many years the scene of such domestic
happiness as God rarely grants on earth; too
rich, indeed, and long-continued already to
be safe for those who would "live by the
faith of the Son of God," and have evidence
of their heavenly adoption; "for what son
is he whom the Father chasteneth not?" ·

But now a shadow was on the dwelling.
This happy household was tasting what has
proved, indeed, "the beginning of sorrows."

He was summoned to the dying bed of
that precious mother, from whom so many
of his gifts were inherited; by whose graceful and tender hand they had been so faith-
fully trained; and by whose pre-eminent holi-

ness and prayerfulness they were unceasingly consecrated to God:

A fortnight after she had "fallen asleep," in a letter to an absent sister, he thus pours out his chastened sorrow : or shall I not rather call it his "song in the night."

"In truth, though it may seem strange, I have had very little to say to anybody since the death of our precious mother. The great thoughts and emotions that fill mind and heart at such times, have not yet begun to frame themselves in words. This does not arise from overwhelming grief. I am seldom otherwise than cheerful. Sometimes, indeed, the thought of never seeing her again in all her various and delightful relations to us, falls like black night upon my soul. But I do not follow it up; and usually I think of her spirit in its present blessedness and glory, and her body as I saw it the night of her death,—the face without a trace of pain, and lighted up by a smile that seemed a ray caught from ' the excellent glory.' I rejoice and thank God for that last view of my mother; and trust I shall bear that face in mind until I see it again, before the Father's throne, in the majesty, grace and beauty of immortality. Indeed this seems to be the prevailing state of mind among us. I had not thought it possible that such a loss could be borne so cheerfully. Sometimes I feel as if we were too cheerful, when our Teacher, Counsellor, Mother lies in the cold grave; is it not due to her to mourn? Then I remember what she was, how she died, what she is now, and what she is doing, and I think it would be grovelling for the children of such a saint to be sad."

Very rich was the baptism of grace and peace, zeal and tenderness, which came down upon his soul, as he lingered for a few weeks by this hallowed grave; and then, having accepted a call for his pastoral services from the Bethlehem Church, in Hanover, he removed thither and entered on his labors.

He was drawn to this position chiefly because of the access it gave him to a multitude of negroes, in this immediate neighborhood, and at Tappahannock, in Essex, where he preached one Sabbath in the month. He had long felt a profound interest in their spiritual welfare; (an interest, let me say, drawn in great part from the soul of his mother); it had engaged his pen and his prayers; and he now rejoiced to "condescend to men of low estate," and, like his Master, "preach the gospel to the poor." From long conversations with him on this subject, I am convinced that he would rather have been honored of God to do a great work among them, than occupy the most conspicuous position in the gift of the Church.

Who that has ever preached to them, especially when gathered in large crowds, has not found his work full of gladness? Their beaming delight in listening to the gospel warmly presented; their devotion to the person and name of Jesus; their perpetual pleasure in the recital of his miracles, love, sufferings and gracious offices; the almost electric response from the whole congregation when their fancy is pleased, or some deeper chord in their experience is struck; the fervor, simplicity and originality of their prayers, often charming the ear by their touching cadences, and melting the heart by their affectionate pathos; the wild modulations and glorious choral swell of their songs; their hearty greetings of him who has warmed them afresh with the love of Christ, as he comes down from the pulpit and offers his hand:—it would be a cold nature indeed, which, amidst such scenes, would not glow with new life, and love, and joy in the gospel of our Lord!

It is almost needless, then, to say that these influences, falling constantly on a soul already inflamed with love to God and man, were most beneficial. His preaching gained boldness and breadth. His manner was more unconstrained. He dealt more directly and fearlessly with the conscience, and learned to abandon himself to the tide of his emotions.

His ministrations were not confined, however, to the servants. One whole Sabbath, every month, and the half of the others, were exclusively theirs; while they could freely participate in the morning services, also, more especially designed for their masters.

These peaceful labors were disturbed by our national troubles. The calamities of his country weighed heavily on his heart. On the day of fasting and prayer in January, 1861, appointed by President Buchanan in view of the storm whose portentous shadows were darkening the land, he said in a letter to one of his family, "I can think of nothing but our beloved country. All day I have wrestled before God in its behalf, and have found peace in being able to commit all its interests to him."

A few months later he writes : "What would we know of the value or strength of our faith, if we were always under summer skies? For the development of godlike character, of faith, humility, courage and self-denial, there are few better scenes and times than those through which we are now passing.

"The South has, though unworthy, been invested with the great privilege of defending the principles of 1776.

"The same phenomena are re-appearing, which astonished the world a century ago. No one around me seems unwilling to come down to real privation, if the State should need the sacrifice. And we are far more united than during the first Revolution. I trust that we shall be purified, elevated and set forward for a grand career.

"My best hope for the North is, that she will emerge from this fire stripped of mobocracy, and under a limited monarchy, or a government so strong as to be republican in name alone. I believe that, with the social condition of the North, a representative republican government, under the constitution of 1788, and on the basis of universal suffrage, is impossible."

With an anxious heart he had watched the encroachments of Northern fanaticism. He saw it agitating in Church and State, trampling on the Bible and the Constitution, cursing men and blaspheming God. He saw it rending the great religious denominations, one by one, pausing only to riot a moment in their discord, and then hastening on, with its eye of greed, its brow of brass, its lips dripping with venom, and its hands only not *yet* dripping with blood!

And THAT he was soon to see. The darkest shadows became darker realities. The war was forced upon us. This sovereign Commonwealth was required to aid in beating down into degradation, and whipping back into servility, her free sisters of the further South, or join with them in their just independence, and throw her generous breast before them, to receive the first blow of the tyrant's rod, and bear the brunt of his wrath. She obeyed her heart, exercised her right, and stood in the breach.

On the 18th of July, in the battle of Bull Run, he saw the heart's blood of his gentle cousin, Major Carter H. Harrison, drawn by Northern bullets on Virginia soil. In three days more, at Manassas, he saw his native soil wet again by the blood of the only nephews of his mother, the only sons of their mother, Holmes and Tucker Conrad, and by the blood of his own pure and beautiful brother, Lieut. Peyton Randolph Harrison. These four young men were all faithful servants of God. Their lives were lovely and useful. In His fear they fought. They were sustained by His grace when they fell. The Conrads were shot at the same moment, and falling side by side, lay, as in the sleep of childhood, almost in each other's arms. The younger of them was nearly ready to begin the ministry of the gospel.

The noble death of these young men stirred the soul of Dabney Harrison to its depth. From the beginning of the war he had longed to share the hardships and dangers of his compatriots. Nothing but his profession held him back for a moment. But now he hesitated no longer. His mind was made up. "I must take my brother's place," he calmly said, and nothing could turn him from that resolve. He left "the quiet and still air of delightful studies," left his loving people and sweet little home in Hanover, and, having raised a company by great personal exertions, entered the service.

It could hardly be expected that all his friends should approve this step. His motives, indeed, were never doubted, though some questioned the wisdom of his decision. They think it wrong for a minister of Jesus ever to take the sword. I shall not undertake to decide between their judgment and his. I know he would have abhorred himself, and repented in dust and ashes, if he had detected any passion for military glory turning him aside from his soul's great aim and end, the service and glory of Christ

Jesus his Lord. I know that he would have fought in no war but one in which his country was repelling invasion, and doing battle for its very hearth-stones and the altars of God. I know that, even then, he would never have taken up the sword, if he must have laid down the Bible; that he would never have become a captain, if he could not also remain a minister. I know that he entered the army devoutly believing that, by this step, his usefulness, even as a preacher of God's word, would be increased.

If ever there was a bosom in which the heart of peace beat with even pulse, it was his. If ever there was a house where an apostle and his benediction might tarry, because "the son of peace was there," that, too, was his. He was a child of "the God of peace," an ambassador of "the Prince of peace," a minister of "the gospel of peace." Peace reigned in his heart; it beamed from his face; it dwelt on his lips. Nothing could disturb it: for it was "the peace of God, which passeth all understanding," and, according to the promise, it "kept" (that is, guarded *) "his heart and mind through

* The original word means etymologically, "to be on the look-out," "to act as a vidette, or signal watchman," or what is now so familiar to us, "a picket-guard." How suggestive as to the position of "God's peace" in its guardianship of the Christian's soul!

Christ Jesus." Whatever the care or cross, however dark the night or rough the storm, this heavenly sunshine in his breast was clear. Under all the provocations of this war, who saw him give way, even for a moment, to a bitter spirit, or heard him speak a word unbecoming a minister of Christ ?— Several months after he entered the service, he said, with thankfulness and joy, that he had not been conscious of one revengeful feeling toward our enemies. No : he would fight for his country; but he would not hate. He durst die, but not sin. Conscience, not passion, made him a soldier; but who does not know that conscience is mightier than passion! His valor was, through the grace of God, without fierceness; but like steel, whose heat has been quenched in cold waters, it was, therefore, all the firmer and keener, of higher polish and more fatal stroke.

He spent three months with his company in the Camp of Instruction, near Richmond. Besides giving himself with ardor to his military duties, he abounded in labors for the souls of the thousands around him.

Of his character and usefulness as a soldier and a Christian, in his new relations, I am enabled to present the following decisive testimony from the pen of an eye-witness. It was prepared, at my request, by my brother, the Rev. Moses D. Hoge, D. D., of Richmond, who, in addition to his pastoral duties in the city, has been serving as Chaplain to that camp, and was in daily intercourse with Captain Harrison during his stay there.

"Since my connection with the Camp of Instruction, I have frequently enjoyed the assistance of pastors of different denominations residing in Richmoud, and of ministers attached to regiments temporarily stationed in the camp.

"Of the latter, Captain Harrison was with us longer than any other clergyman in the service, and he delighted to avail himself of every opportunity of aiding me in my important work.

"In addition to daily visits to the sick in the hospitals, I had three appointments each week for preaching in the camp; and whenever I was prevented by any cause from meeting these engagements, he was always ready to take my place; and I had the most abundant evidence of the efficiency of his labors, and of the gratitude of the men for his efforts to promote their temporal and spiritual welfare.

" His gentleness and sympathy; his facility in adapting his instructions to the characters and capacities of the sick, and the unction that gave such a charm to his prayers, always rendered him a welcome visitor to the Hospital, and made him the instrument both of profit and consolation.

"During the summer, several thousand troops were sometimes stationed at once in our camp, and Captain Harrison was, of course, brought into contact with a large number of officers. Over these he experienced the most happy influence.

"While no man was more inflexible in his adherence to his convictions of duty, or more prompt to rebuke whatever he believed to be wrong in principle or in conduct, yet his manner was so conciliating; such was the candor and kindness of his disposition; such his scrupulous respect for the rights, and regard for the feelings of others, that he rarely gave offence, even when he attempted to repress what he deemed culpable. The very presence of one so frank and fearless in his bearing, so delicate and refined in his tastes, so pure and elevated in his principles, was ordinarily sufficient to check any exhibitions of profanity or vulgarity. And, withal, he was so genial in his nature, so entertaining in his conversation, and obliging in his disposition, that his presence was never regarded as imposing an irksome restraint, even in a company of the irreligious.

"A striking illustration of his self-possession and insensibility to fear occurred, very unexpectedly, one day during his stay in our camp.

"An altercation took place between a few members of two regiments, stationed not far from each other, which resulted in the serious wounding of one of the men. In a few moments a large number in both regiments took up the quarrel. Several companies rushed, arms in hand, to the scene of the *melee*, and stood confronting each other, ready to engage in what threatened to become a bloody strife. Colonel, now General, Dimmock, then Commandant of the Post, was providentially passing at the moment, and Captain Harrison also, and they ran between the exasperated lines, and kept them asunder. Captain Harrison at once assumed an authority to which he had no official right, and yet one whose moral force was quickly felt; and by means of his expostulations and commands, addressed chiefly to the officers on either side, he gave such efficient co-operation to General Dimmock, as to constrain the belligerents to separate, and withdraw to their several quarters.— Thus, what began as a brawl, but came near ending as a battle, was promptly and finally suppressed.

"One of the most interesting incidents

connected with Captain Harrison's sojourn in our camp, was his success in forming a "Young Men's Christian Association" in the regiment* to which his company was attached. The organization was as complete and thorough as that of any similar association in town or city. It had the usual number of officers and committees for conducting prayer-meetings, distributing religious publications, and providing teachers for the Sabbath school and Bible classes. No one, unfamiliar with camp-life, can fully appreciate the value of such an association in counteracting the demoralization so common among men exposed to such temptations as soldiers are, and deprived too of those domestic, social and religious influences, which, like guardian angels, hovered around them in their own homes. A chaplain, whether at a post or in a regiment, can have no ally comparable to a well organized and efficiently managed Christian Association among the men to whom he ministers. It is not only an instrument of incalculable good to the irreligious, but one of the best means of keeping alive the spirituality, and of developing the Christian graces of the pious officers and men who become enlisted in its work as active members.

---

* The Fifty-Sixth Regiment of Virginia Volunteers.

"If others have shown
   '——how awful goodness is—— '
it was Dabney Harrison's happy province to show how amiable and attractive it may appear, when thus illustrated in the life of a Christrian gentleman and soldier. While he remained in our camp, he moved about as one whose superiority was tacitly acknowledged without exciting ill-will or envy; and when he left us, he was regretted as one whose place was not to be filled again. Since the commencement of this war, my position has brought me in contact with many of the officers in our army, but I have known few equal, and none superior, to my lamented friend, in the possession of those gifts and graces which impart true nobility to the man, and attractive loveliness to the Christian.

"When the startling telegram came, announcing his death, I felt and said, as doubtless so many others did, that when the particulars of the event should reach us, they would be such as to fill the heart of every friend with just pride, and such as would show to the world how gloriously a Christian soldier could die for the sacred cause to which he had consecrated his all.

"So far as the fulfilment of all these expectations is concerned, there is nothing left

B

to wish ; for in all this war, and in all past wars, I believe no record can be found of two brothers whose fall was characterized by more that is calculated to awaken sentiments of reverential admiration. Examples like theirs illustrate whatever is noblest and most worthy of perpetual remembrance in the annals of a people battling for liberty and right. How precious must ever be the independence which is won by such sacrifices!"

While Captain Harrison's heart and work extended to the surrounding multitudes, it is only just to say that his first anxiety was for his own men. He had gathered them and given them to the service. They were to follow him, it might be to the death. He was their Captain, and so was in closer relation to them than was possible for any other officer. They, of all others, would see what he actually was, as a servant of his country, as a servant of his God. Should *he* be self-indulgent, querulous, faint-hearted, indifferent to discipline, insubordinate to his superiors, what could he expect of them ?

Therefore he sought to be, every day and in everything, an example to them. He shared their hardships, and all so cheerfully, that the most despondent could hardly fail to catch some quickening ray from his sunny spirit. As far as was possible, too, he made them share any comfort pertaining to his position. While his discipline was firm, his sorrow that they should need it was so manifest, that their hearts were drawn out in new love to him, and they tried ever after to do right for his sake. The inexperienced found in him a faithful guardian, the perplexed went to him freely for counsel, and all the company felt that in him they had not only a brave and vigilant commander, but a true friend.

As they were under him, he remembered that he was answerable for them. After a battle his country might say to him, "You held a Captain's commission. A company of men was entrusted to your care. Your problem was; how to produce, in a given time, from a given number of men having such and such capacities, the greatest aggregate of military efficiency. How have you solved it? How much of the responsibility of this day's losses, how much of the glory of this day's successes, belongs to you?"— Therefore he labored steadfastly to make the most of his company,—to make the most of each man, and set him in the field in his best plight, with the best preparation, and both urged and upheld by the best principles.

And what were those principles? The profoundest of all writers shall answer. After celebrating the heroic patience and valor of the grandest statesman and commander of antiquity, he lays bare the secret springs of his power in these words: "He endured as seeing Him who is invisible." How *can* any principle of action be so fruitful in all that is great and good, as faith in God,— living faith in that Being who alone is infinite in greatness and goodness! To dwell consciously in His immediate presence, and under His all-beholding eye; to act in view of His judgment throne, and therefore to strive to "do always those things that please Him;" to enjoy His gracious friendship; to be assured of His sympathy in every sorrow, and His help in every difficulty; to labor by day, and lie down by night under His smile; yea, to enter into a new and lofty relationship with Him, and be filled with a new and nobler life: must not these things tell with great and salutary power upon the character? Every man, not abandoned to impudence, acts carefully in the presence of others. But an enlightened conscience is a perpetual witness, before which the soul must needs be virtuous; or, as an old writer expresses it, "Conscience is as a thousand witnesses;" and then, rising higher in the scale of controlling influences, he declares with an energy which is only just, that "the all-seeing God is as a thousand con-sciences."

But does not the great poet of human na-ture tell us that "Conscience does make cowards of us all?" Yes, it does and ought to hold us back when we would do wrong. But when we do right; when the path of danger is also the path of duty; when we draw the sword in righteous war; then, with Coleridge, we may turn the sentiment, and cry out, "but oh! it is conscience too which makes heroes of us all!" Or with Shaks-peare himself we may exclaim,

"What stronger breast-plate than a heart un-tainted?
Thrice is he arm'd, that hath his quarrel just!"

Was not Captain Harrison wise, then, in trying to bring his men to fear God? Was it not a patriotic as well as a Christian duty? When, by preaching the gospel of the Lord Jesus, he strove to prepare his men for the retributions which lie beyond the grave, was he not equally preparing them for the res-ponsibilities which lie on this side of it? If a whole army were sober, patient, content; if every man were vigilant, courageous and full of zeal; if "the awful idea of accountability " waited on authority, and rose with the rank; while the humblest private esteemed it honor and dignity enough to obey without questioning, and stand in his lot without flinching; would not that army be full of the stuff of which victories are made? And does not the gospel enjoin all these virtues? Yea, does it not supply them, too, as nothing else ever can? Supply them to all who seek them with an honest, earnest, believing heart? Then, in preaching the gospel to his men, was not this army officer doing military service most direct and excellent?*

If these things are true, then another thing is false; that foul maxim, namely, which has run so long a career of mischief, "the worse the man, the better the soldier!" It is false, or all war is wickedness, and every good soldier is a bad man, and the best soldier is a villian. It is false, or all those attributes and deeds, by which liberty has been won and right maintained, ought no more to thrill our hearts and moisten our eyes; they should be abhorred, and consigned to infamy.

---

* "The virtue and fidelity which should characerize a soldier, can be learned from the holy pages of the Bible alone."—General Robert E. Lee.

Here I crave room in behalf of virtuous and godly men in great numbers, fallen or yet fighting in our righteous cause; in behalf also of ignorant and tempted men; to plead a little further against this odious slander on all true heroism. False and foolish as it is, it has no small share in the corruptions prevalent in almost every army.— Vicious men, besides making it both a cloak and spur for their vices, have used it to frighten the green recruit into premature ripeness in sin, as his only way to soldierly renown. With what result, let Cowper's picture of the returned soldier show.

"To swear, to game, to drink, to show at home
By lewdness, idleness and Sabbath-breaking,
The great proficiency he made abroad,
T'astonish and to grieve his gazing friends,
To break some maiden's and his mother's heart,
To be a pest where he was useful once,
Are his sole aim, and all his glory now·"

"Sir Alexander Ball," says Coleridge in his exquisite biographical sketch of that distinguished British Admiral, the honored and special friend of Lord Nelson, "Sir Alexander Ball quoted the speech of an old admiral, one of whose two great wishes was to have a ship's crew composed altogether of serious Scotchmen. He spoke with great reprobation of the vulgar notion, 'the worse man, the better sailor.' Courage, he said, was the natural product of familiarity with danger, while thoughtlessness would often-times turn into fool-hardiness; and that he had always found the most usefully brave sailors the greatest and most rational of his crew. The best sailor he ever had . . . . . . was never heard to swear an oath, and was remarkable for the firmness with which he devoted a part of every Sunday to the reading of his Bible." "I record this," adds Coleridge, "with satisfaction as a testimony of great weight, and in all respects unexceptionable."

"I have often heard it said," wrote Hedley Vicars, 'The worse the man, the better the soldier!' "Facts contradict this untruth. Were I ever, as the leader of a forlorn hope, allowed to select my men, it would be most certainly from among the soldiers of Christ; for who should fight so fearlessly and bravely, as those to whom death presents no after terrors?"*

But not with words alone did Hedley Vicars bear witness. Far clearer is the utterance of his eloquent life. Would that every soldier in our army could read the charming narrative! Who that has, does not feel his heart kindling into new warmth and resolu-

---

* Memorials of Captain Hedley Vicars, p. 117.

tion, as he recalls his generous nature, his abounding usefulness, and the touching beauty of his victorious death?

But need I multiply testimony on a subject like this? Tell me, my countrymen, does an immortal man go best into battle with an oath or a prayer on his lips? With snatches of a lewd ballad suddenly scared from his memory, or with the grand measures of some brave old psalm still ringing through his soul and bracing his frame?— With the senses blunted and the brain dizzy with the fumes of a recent debauch, or with all his faculties kept clear by temperance, firm by exercise, and bright with the smile of an approving conscience and an approving God?

If this be a digression, it matters little. In such a day as this, we are all rather waiting to hail any re-enforcements to truth, than critical as to the order of their coming in.

But I do not feel that I have turned aside for a moment from my chief purpose. All the while as I write, "the voice of my brother's blood crieth unto me." From the far-off banks of the Cumberland it utters its testimony, "He, being dead, yet speaketh." He has taken his place in that bright overshadowing "cloud of witnesses," whose testimony gathers so luminously around this truth,—that a hearty faith in God is the best preparation for "the life that now is," and for "that which is to come."

Let us thank God that "we are compassed about with so great a cloud of witnesses" to so glorious a truth. "The time would fail me to tell of" those elder heroes, patriots and martyrs in God's great witnessing army, who in the might of faith, "subdued kingdoms, wrought righteousness, obtained promises, stopped the mouths of lions, quenched the violence of fire, escaped the edge of the sword, out of weakness were made strong, waxed valiant in fight, turned to flight the armies of the aliens;" "of whom the world was not worthy." They have been raised up in all ages. Our own day has been greatly honored. Such men as Havelock in India, whom Lord Hardinge pronounced "every inch a soldier, and every inch a Christian," Hedley Vicars in the Crimea, and Dabney Harrison in our own Confederacy, do not stand alone. Each one of them is the representative of a "goodly fellowship" in "precious faith" and achievement answerable thereto. One died "in the fulness of all his powers, in the rich autumn of ripe yet undecaying manhood." The others were cut off in the golden prime of their fruitful summer. But they were all soldiers in the same great army, and, "according to the grace given them," they "fought a good fight," they "finished their course," they "kept the faith."

It is unnecessary to dwell on the hardships of Captain Harrison's winter campaign in the West;—hard fare and harder lodging, and constant exposure to the wet and cold. Whatever he bore, many thousands bore with him; and there are multitudes of whom that may be said, which is so true of him; no one ever saw him falter, no one ever heard him murmur. A brief extract from one of his letters may serve to show the pleasant spirit in which all these privations and annoyances were met.

BOWLING GREEN, KENTUCKY, }
January 18, 1862. }

"MY DEAR FATHER: I have been forcibly reminded, to-day, of an incident in Ruxton's travels. Out on a prairie, he found a wretched looking man, all alone, in a pouring rain, stooping over a few smouldering embers, and singing,

'How happy are we,
Who from care are free!
Oh! why are not all
Contented like me?'

"My tent is on a hill-side, and has a flue instead of a chimney. It rained hard all last night, has rained all of to-day, and is raining yet. The water has risen in my tent, the fire has been drowned out, the floor is nearly all mud, and I have been writing all the morning, in a chair stuck deep in this mud. My bed is kept out of it by some fence-rails, and my larder is a basket on the ground at the bed's head, containing a piece of pork and a bag of flour. There is not a negro in Virginia that would not despise such lodgings. But I am 'contented.' I sleep soundly, work hard, eat heartly, and am fattening."

A day or two later he writes: "I have just finished a large stone chimney to my tent, and shall have it floored with poles to-morrow; then I shall be in great state!"

But this life had, now and then, a charming interruption. His letters speak gratefully of kindness and hospitality at almost every stopping-place. They make special mention of Lynchburg, where his ever faithful and honored friend, "good Captain McCorkle" took him in charge; Wytheville, where a gentleman came out and loaded him with benefits; Abingdon, where he "was asked at once to delightful quarters at the Martha Washington Institute," and "made entirely at home" by the Rev. Mr. Harris, its principal; and Russelville, Kentucky, where, having begun a letter, almost sick, and sitting on a stone, out in the fast-falling sleet, he ended it before a blazing fire, in his luxurious chamber in the house of some of his kindred, now met for the first time.

After entering the service, his heart never wavered. To one who urged doubts as to the propriety of his course, he thus replies; "I am honestly and earnestly engaged in a great work. The causes of discouragement as to my ministerial usefulness are, I confess, very great; yet I hope I have done *some* good. I never felt more convinced that it is incumbent on me to do this work. I did not expect comfort when I entered on it, and I have not been disappointed. But a great opportunity for performing and enduring in the service of God and my country I have found, and I do not regret it."

He speaks modestly when he says he hopes he has done *some* good. His usefulness was a continual dew. It is not possible to estimate the precious influence which constantly streamed, not only from his special essays to do good, but from his whole life and his very presence. Some of his men were addicted to profane swearing; but when they saw how their Captain was grieved by it, they either abandoned the habit, or were careful never to offend where he could hear. And to how many did he give altogether new impressions of the religion of our Lord Jesus, when they saw how beautifully innocence could blend with wisdom; how the very purity of woman could consist with the valor of man, just as whiteness and enduring substance are combined in marble; and how the most uncompromising godliness could be inwoven with the elegance of the gentleman, while the devoutest piety but gave new fire to the ardor of the patriot!

And may we not hope that many, who as they looked on him felt that "wisdom's ways are," indeed, "ways of pleasantness," and that "all her paths are peace," will not rest till they are themselves walking therein? That they who were charmed with "the beauty of holiness" as it shone in him, will seek for it, and find it, as he did, in the imitation of Jesus?

A few days ago an intelligent gentleman, while conversing with me about him, suddenly exclaimed with tears, "O! sir, I never could look in that man's face without thinking of our Saviour!" Would that this might be the thought first awakened in the minds of all who knew him as they recall his image; and that they also, who know him only from this imperfect sketch, might be led to look with adoring contemplation on the face of his blessed Master! To Him belongs all the glory of whatever was excellent in His servant. Oh, how exceeding fair must HE be, when He can thus beautify our vile nature! The following extracts show Capt. Harrison's faithful devotion to his men, and how, even in these stormy times, God sometimes rewarded his spiritual husbandry with heavenly fruit: "After a weary day, I settled down for the night to nurse my good old Sergeant Jones. His life is despaired of. I am much attached to him, and was glad to wait on him. I have for some time been striving to bring him to Christ, and I should not be without hope in his death."

A day or two later; "My good old Sergeant is gone. Two evenings before his death, he held my hand for a long time, and said he loved me very much as God's instrument for good to him. I trust it may be true."

For those who saw with admiration his constant cheerfulness after his sore bereavement at Manassas, I cannot forbear drawing the veil a little aside, that they may look into his heart, and see what the burden was, which for Christ and his country's sake, he thus carried. "In truth," he writes a few weeks before his death, "one great grief is so constantly upon my heart, that it drives out selfish sorrow. I cannot get over the loss of my brother; my noble, charming, gallant, godly brother. Love and admiration for his person; delight in his society and conversation; pride in his great, tender soul, wondrous gifts, high character and success; and hopes for a future of increasing usefulness and happiness;---all dashed at one fell blow! I submit to it; for him I rejoice in it; but I can not get used to it. I believe I shall miss him constantly and sorrowfully, as long as I live. I am not sad; even now, when deprived of my wife and little ones. But I feel as if I would rather be serious the rest of my life. I am glad you told me of your Christmas. Had I been present at your morning worship, I expect I should have wept too; my tears lie almost as shallow now, as when I was a child."

Shortly after, he thus writes to one who had recently confessed Christ, and on whose young heart the same "great grief" was lying, while heavy strokes were soon to fall in swift succession: "If sorrow weans us from the world, and makes heaven look bright; if it humbles our pride, and makes us cling to Christ; it is not to be repented of. I am glad to see that your trouble does not take the turn of doubting your acceptance with God. Never let it do that! We have suffered irreparble losses; it is right to weep over them. We are deeply sinful; it is right to mourn for that. But the question of our hope involves the faithfulness of God, and the truth of our Lord Jesus Christ, who has promised that we shall "never perish," "neither shall any pluck" us "out of His hand."

"I never feel anything now that I can call merriment, or gaeity of spirit. The vision of those fresh graves is too clear; the wounds of those terrible blows are too deep; and all my loved ones are too far away; and the time is altogether too dark and troublous.

"But on the other hand I am rarely, and never long, cast down. How can I be, with God's promises so bright, and His word so true, and His mercies so rich and free, when I think of the joy of our loved ones on high When I think of the good that may come to unborn generations by our present priva tions? Let us trust, and pray, and hope to the end. The glory that awaits us outweighs all the troubles that surround us."

Thus from his own bleeding heart was a balm distilled for the wounds of others; and thus was that sweet Scripture fulfilled, "The God of all comfort comforteth us in all our tribulation, that we may be able to

B 2

comfort them which are in any trouble, by the comfort wherewith we ourselves are comforted of God."

His own " consolation," meanwhile, " abounded by Christ," and his hope was brightening with light from the open gates of the City. " I have much personal enjoyment of religion, he writes. _" I feel driven near to God, and I love to commune with Him. I cannot imagine how people, who do not love and serve Him, keep up heart in times of separation and sorrow like thsse. I feel more thankful and amazed at His wondrous love, every time I think of it. We know not what is before us; but we do know that we have a gracious Father, and a blessed Mercy-seat."

On Monday night, February 10th, six days before his death, he thus closes a long letter from the camp before Fort Donelson : " Oh, how all these adventures, with their perils and deliverances, their privations and blessings, do drive us to our God! I want no other strength than the Lord Jehovah; no other Redeemer than our blessed Saviour; no other Comforter than His Holy Spirit. I believe that when we do our duty, the Lord will fight for us. I feel a constant, bright and cheering trust in Him. I think of my precious wife and little ones, and long for

their society and caresses, but I am satisfied that it is right that I should be here, and I await the development of His will. ......
"I think His mercy in making us His children in spite of all our ill-desert, ought to make us willing meekly to bear all that He chooses to lay upon us."

When this lofty yet tender confession of his faith had been put on record, he wrote two playful letters to be read to his little daughter and son, and laid down the pen, from which we had hoped that, for many years to come, gracious streams should flow to "make glad the City of God." It was, indeed, taken up once more for a moment; but the hand that held it was growing cold, and it was laid aside forever.

Mightily as many earthly loves drew upon his soul, his Lord's love was more than all. He had "prepared a place" for him "in his Father's House," and now He desired his coming. Beyond the river, and before the throne, His voice was heard saying, "Father, I will that they whom Thou hast given Me, be with Me, where I am, that they may behold My glory." And then from Mount Zion, which is above, came words which once sounded in thunder from Mount Sinai; but now they came softly, and were unheard by any mortal ear. They were words of discharge and blessing, breathed in music that night over the pillow of the sleeping soldier: "Six days shalt thou labor and do all thy work; but the seventh is the Sabbath of the Lord thy God."

Six days for earth and labor; only six.— Then his eternal Sabbath would begin; rest and worship and joy forever!

It was my sad privilege very lately to spend some hours with the little remnant of his cherished company, and read them part of this narrative. Their love, admiration and grief for their lost Captain seemed to have no measure. Now they wept like children, now their faces beamed with enthusiasm, and now they broke in upon my story with hearty confirmations and additions. They gave me minute accounts of these last days, but I shall not detain my reader with many details. It was 'a week of exposure, peril, exhausting toils and almost unbroken sleeplessness. The battle of Fort Donelson began on Wednesday. That night was spent in throwing up breastworks. His men say that no man in the company worked harder, or did more in this heavy labor than "the Captain." Thursday night was cold and stormy. The rain fell in torrents on the weary watchers in the trenches, and, soon changing into sleet, their clothes froze upon them. By Friday evening, Captain Harrison's frame, never robust, gave way for a time, and he was compelled to retire to the Hospital, where he lay quite sick all that night. Yet on Saturday morning, a great while before day, and against the remonstrances of his friends, he rose and returned to his command.

The officer, who commanded the Fifty-Sixth Regiment at this time, gave me several instances of such zeal and daring on the part of Captain Harrison, that I cannot refrain from applying to him what Clarendon says of "that incomparable young man, Lord Falkland," in his touching account of his death : " He had a courage of the most clear and keen temper, and so far from fear, that he seemed not without some appetite of danger."

" You ought to be braver than the rest of us," said some of his brother officers to him one day, after witnessing some exhibition of his serene fearlessness in danger.

" Why so ?" said he pleasantly.

" Because," said they, " you have everything settled for eternity. You have nothing to fear after death."

" Well, gentlemen," said he solemnly, after a moment's pause, " you are right.— Everything *is* settled, I trust, for eternity, and I have nothing to fear."

It was his invariable custom to gather his men every morning and evening for "family prayers." A letter in one of our daily papers contains a notice of one of these services. It was on Thursday morning, just after the night of heavy toil in throwing up breastworks. Before it was light enough to read, Captain Harrison called on his men to rest a while, and join him in worshipping God. They came, and a large portion of the regiment with them, crowding closely around him. He then repeated, says this writer, with thrilling effect, the twenty-seventh Psalm, and led them in prayer with great fervor and power. He speaks of the whole scene as most impressive.

How could it be otherwise? These men were soon to face the terrors of death; some of them were to taste its bitterness; and now they stood with their Pastor and Captain in this grand temple of the open heavens, that he might first present them before God, and commend them to His grace.

As the full moon, which had shone upon their labor all night, was sinking in the west, and the "light" of that "morning without clouds" appeared faintly above the eastern hills, this sublime strain of the ancient Hebrew warrior and poet fell on their ears,

"The Lord is my light and my salvation; whom shall I fear? The Lord is the strength of my life; of whom shall I be afraid?"

As the columns of the enemy's force, horse and foot, were seen coming onward in the distance, this outburst of courage and faith stirred their souls like the sound of a clarion; "Though an host should encamp against me, my heart shall not fear! Though war should rise against me, in this will I be confident!"

As he uttered the words, "When Thou saidst, Seek ye My face; my heart said unto Thee, Thy face, Lord, will I seek," who can describe the satisfaction *they* must have felt, who remembered that with all the heart they had thus responded to God's gracious invitation?

At the words, "When my father and my mother forsake me," if some grew faint with thoughts of home far distant, and loving parents who could not be near in the honr of sorest need, did they not revive again as they heard the promise, "then the Lord will take me up?"

And how inspiring to men about to do battle in the righteous cause, the exhortation which closes the Psalm: "Wait on the Lord! Be of good courage, and He shall strengthen thine heart! Wait, I say, on the Lord!"

Saturday was his fifth and great day of "work," work of war, work of suffering.— For "now he was ready to be offered, and the time of his departure was at hand."— This gentle "Barnabas, son of consolation," was to show that he was also, like the beloved Disciple whom he so much resembled, "Boanerges, son of thunder." As the sun rose on the morning of that bloody day, it saw him enter the thick of the battle, and wrestle valiantly with the foe. With dauntless heart he cheered on his men. They eagerly followed wherever he led. Their testimony is, that he never said, "Go on," but always, "Come on," while ever before them flashed his waiving sword. At length with fear and pain they saw his firm step faltering, his erect form wavering. He fell, and the fierce tide of battle swept on. It was impossible for his most devoted men to pause. And they best did his will by passing over his prostrate body, throwing themselves on the foe, and leaving him to die. "He had warred a good warfare, ever holding faith and a good conscience."

With reverence I have taken in my hand the hat he wore in the battle; with tears and a swelling heart I have gazed on it. It is pierced by four balls. Three whistled through and did him no harm. The fourth, partly spent, marred that beautiful brow. But this was as nothing. He calmly fought on. A more deadly aim drove a ball through his right lung. Just when, cannot be told. His face was to the foe, and his step onward, even when from loss of blood and exhaustion, he sank upon the frozen earth.

There, with his head resting on a log, he lay unattended for an hour and a half, suffering from his wounds, but more from the chill air and his bed of snow. When at length his men were ordered to cease their fire, they hastened to his side. They found him almost numb with the cold. Yet he met them pleasantly, and told them not to mind him, that he must die whatever was done, and that he would rather they would take care of themselves.' "We could not have left him then," said one of his faithful men with a burst of honest enthusiasm, "if all the regiments of the enemy had been after us!" They made a litter, and six of them bore him to Dover, a little village hard by the battle-field.

Here they placed him by a good fire, rubbed his cold limbs, and put hot bricks to his feet. As soon as he was warm, he said,— "Now I am perfectly comfortable;" and from this time, though his consciousness was perfect, and every faculty bright, he had

B 3

neither pain nor uneasiness. He had done with suffering forever. Neither had he the least desire for food, though he had fasted since the evening before. Nor did he even sleep again, except for a few minutes shortly before his death, although he had yet some thirty-six hours to live. An occasional draught of cold water supplied all his need.

He conversed cheerfully and without weariness with all who were near him, even to the last.

After a few hours, he was put on a steamboat for Nashville. When he found that two of his men were to go with him and wait upon him, he remonstrated for a while. He was unwilling that an arm, that could still strike in the cause for which he had poured out his life, should be employed in ministering to any needs of his. But when he saw that they would not leave him, he gave expression to his great desire to sleep on Virginia soil; or, if that could not be, he wished to be laid to rest as near to it as possible.

While bearing their precious charge to the boat, a touching incident occurred. I shall give it in the words of Lieut. Col. Massie, who commanded the 51st Regiment of Virginia Volunteers. It was kindly furnished me by one of his faimily, from a private letter, with permission to use his name. "Poor Dabney Harrison was killed,—another of that patriotic family. . . . . I believed him to be the most thorough gentleman I had ever known. . . . . After the battle, and while I was sitting on my horse, some one said, 'Colonel, the Captain says, Good-bye!' I saw a litter passing, and immediately dismounted and stopped it, and you may better imagine than I describe my feelings, when I found poor Harrison, calm, pale, with the same sweet smile, lying shot through the lungs. He said, 'It is all right! I am perfectly willing to die.' 'It is true,' said he, 'I grieve to leave my wife and little children; but they need not fear; God will take care of them.' All the battle has not made so deep an impression on me as that man's death. I cannot account for my tenderness of feeling for him. . . . . He was a daring man, keen for a fight, and was cheering on his men, with hat in hand, at the time he was shot."

Who that knew him, cannot see that "same sweet smile," and hear the cheerful, silver ring of his quick assurance, "It is all right!" Neither the frosts of winter nor the frosts of death could freeze the sunny fountain of that smile; and however bitter the cup of pain and grief put into his hands by his heavenly Father, he would still say as he drank, "It is all right!"

Two incidents of his dying hours are yet to be recorded. Calling, about noon, for one of his manuscript books, he took a pencil, and with a trembling hand feebly wrote these words:

"FEB. 16, 1862.—SUNDAY.

"I die content and happy; trusting in the merits of my Saviour, Jesus; committing my wife and children to their Father and mine.

DABNEY CARR HARRISON."

Precious legacy of love and prayer! Precious testimony of faith and blessedness!

A little while before he died, he slept quietly for a few minutes. In dreams his soul wandered back to yesterday's conflict. He was again in the battle. The company for which he had toiled and prayed and suffered so much was before him, and he was wounded,—dying on the field. But even in dreams he had not lost

"th' unconquerable will,
And courage never to submit or yield."

Starting out of sleep, he sat once more erect, and exclaimed, "Company K, you have no Captain now; but never give up! never surrender!"

The arms of his faithful attendant received him as he rose, and now supported him tenderly as his drooping form grew heavier. With his head pillowed on a soldier's breast, he sank, peacefully as a babe, into that sleep which no visions of strife shall ever disturb.

Once more "the same sweet smile" shone forth, now lighting up that chaste and marble beauty which nothing gives but death.

His work was done, all done, well done, and now, like his brother seven months before, like his sister seven days after, like the little one to whom we had given his name, he died, as he was born, on the Sabbath.— Thus was his life bounded on either hand by the Day of God. Care and conflict came between, but a Sabbath blessing was on it all, and then he entered on the higher "Sabbath of the Lord his God," "eternal in the heavens."

His last breath was for his country; for the young Confederacy, whose liberty, honor and righteousness were inexpressibly dear to him; for which he wept and made supplication in secret; for which he was content to "endure hardness as a good soldier; for which he cheerfully died."

His dying words beautifully connect themselves with those of his brother on the plains of Manassas.

When the Second Virginia Regiment, fighting on our left at Manassas, was broken by a sudden and destructive flank fire of the enemy, and by its Colonel's unfortunate command, Lieut. Peyton Harrison and a few officers of like spirit rallied a portion of the men, and led them in a perilous, but splendid and victorious charge. In the midst of it, however, he fell, shot like his brother, in the breast. Two of his men bore him from the field. His face was radiant with heavenly peace. He spent a few moments in dictating messages of love, and in prayer for himself, his family, and his country. "What more can we do for you?" asked the affectionate young men who supported him.— "Lay me down," was his answer, " I am ready to die; you can do no more for me: rally to the charge!"

"Rally to the charge!" cries the voice from Manassas. "Never give up! never surrender!" answers the voice from Fort Donelson.

Nobly has the land responded to the first cry. By hundreds of thousands have they "rallied" to their country's standard. May they equally heed the second cry! May they "never give up" the sacred struggle! May they "never surrender" their liberty or their land, the homes of the living and the graves of the dead! The blood of our fallen patriots consecrates the cause and the soil. To yield would be treason to the dead.

It is hard to think of that gentle breast pierced with deadly balls. It is hard to bury him in darkness; to look no more upon that slender form, that fair open brow, shaded by rich clusters of brown hair, prematurely touched with silver, that serene but radiant blue eye, that firm sweet mouth, that winning smile; but "even so, Father, for so it seemed good in Thy sight!" We bow to Thy sovereign will, and reverently lay Thy faithful servant in the dust.

It is pleasant to think that, while he sleeps in his lonely grave, far from kindred and friends, he lies wrapped in the martial cloak his sainted brother wore. One in heart, one in aim, they were one in glorious martyrdom. "And devout men made great lamentation over them."